Wings of Fancy

Flairs and Glairs

Publication House

"Wings of Fancy"

ISBN No: 978-93-90799-04-6"
1st Edition
Language – English and Hindi

Flairs and Glairs
Publication House
Regd. Under MSME Act.

Disclaimer

This is a work of fiction and solely represent the thoughts of the corresponding authors of the articles. Our editors have tried their best to edit the content of all the authors and check the plagiarism.

All the write-ups in this book are unique and are only published in this book.

In case any plagiarism or error is found, only the author is responsible alone, and not the publisher or the Compilers.

Cover Designing and Book Formatting
Shubham Shah and Ishani Agarwal

Co Author

Shubham Shah (Founder Flairs and Glairs)
Ishani Agarwal (Co-Founder Flairs and Glairs)
Ms. Ishrat Jahan Noormohammed Khan (Project Coordinator)
Sandhya A.S.(Compiler)

1. Anupriya Vijayan
2. Sruthi Suthesan
3. Sheeba G.
4. Dr. Sreeja S. Nayar
5. Resmi T.R.
6. Vismaya Vijay
7. Madhu Sharma
8. Remya R.G.
9. Rohini K. Potti
10. Anjana S.
11. Fathima Nazeerudeen
12. Maanoj S.
13. Kiruba Jacob
14. Anupa C.S.
15. Aparna Prasad
16. Himamol S.
17. Dr. Aswathy Rajan
18. Kavitha Kaladharan
19. Nikita John
20. Mathew M. George
21. Rekha Nair K.

22. Dr. Anuja Raj
23. Shelma Jayan
24. Dr. Annapoorna Iyer
25. Sandra S.
26. Naima Akhter Lina
27. Arya A.
28. Arsha S. Pillai
29. Shine J.S.
30. Keerthana Rajeev
31. Nayim Nasar P.
32. Aravind S.S.
33. Sachin Jose Mattam
34. Aleena K. Benny
35. Sulfath Seenath
36. Shalu Rahesh
37. Arsha P.
38. Neetha Prasad
39. Ketan Bandu Jadhav
40. Dilip Bhise

Shubham Shah

(Founder- Flairs and Glairs)

Shubham Shah, an entrepreneur at "Flairs & Glairs" a brand with dynamics in events organizing and cultural educational pan INDIA, is a 26yrs old guy who recently has entered the digital platform of imprinting emotions. He has initiated with

his own open mic platform to help budding poets and aspiring writers under his brand named as "Teekhe Zasbaaat"

He is a commerce graduate from the Bhagalpur City of Bihar. He states Writing has impersonated him since childhood and he has now been writing for over a decade!

Cooking, on the other hand, is his passion! He also mentions, trying out new things just tickles him!

When asked sir, Why SPICY EMOTIONS?

He smiled and added, "agar jasbaat teekhe na ho toh wo jasbaat kahan" Spices are all that blends! So do his words!

As a chef, he presents to you his dish! Hot and freshly served! Taste it! Feel it! Enjoy it! You can also find his writing in the Book "Teekhe Zasbaaat" and 50+ Co-authored anthologies. With his passion to explore opportunities across Platforms, he is working with keen devotion and We wish him all the very best for his future ventures.

He is Featured in the **International Magazine De-Mode** for his upcoming solo novel.

He is **Approved by Ne8x for its Lit Fest,** and is a **Golden Star Awards 2020 Winner.**

He is an **India Book of Records Holder** for his Anthology **Satrang,** and has the **Grandmaster** title by **Asia Book of Records**, for the same.

He has also been featured in **Prabhat Khabar, Dainik Jagran** and other renowned Newspaper for his achievements. He has also been awarded with **India Star Republic Award 2021.**

He has been a proud co-author to

India Book of Records (Title- Black)

World Book of Records (Title -15 Wonders of Poetries)

India Book of Records (Title - Aaina)

Vajra World Records Holder (Title - Gustakhi Maaf Hai)

High Range of Records Holder (Title - Gustakhi Maaf Hai)

Share your reviews on his

INSTAGRAM
@spicy_emotions
@shubham4shah
Or via email on
shubham2shah@gmail.com

To stay tuned to his work and opportunities follow his business
Handles

INSTAGRAM   FACEBOOK   YOUTUBE

@flairsandglairs
@teekhezasbaaat

WEBSITE:
https://flairsandglairs.in/
https://flairsandglairs.com/

Ishani Agarwal

(Co-Founder- Flairs and Glairs)

Ishani Agarwal hails from the City of Joy, Kolkata.
She is the co-founder of her Community "Teekhe Zasbaaat" and Flairs and Glairs Publication.
Been a Compiler for 45+ Anthologies, she is in the process for more. Co-authored in 150+ Anthologies. She is a India Book of Records Holder, a Vajra World Records Holder, a High Range of Records Holder and a Bravo Record holder.

Approved by Ne8x for its Lit Fest 2020, and Literary Icon 2020. Also a Golden Star Awards Winner 2020.

She has also been awarded with India Star Republic Award 2021.

She has been featured by the National Magazine "Taree Zameen Par" with the title 'unstoppable'.

Also featured in the International Magazine DeMode for her upcoming solo novel, she is proud to write on social issues, and is happy with the love she is receiving.

Connect with her on Instagram: @Ishani_agarwal_quotes / @compilations_so_far

Ms. Ishrat Jahan Noormohammed Khan
(Project Coordinator)

Ms Ishrat Jahan Khan holds 15 years of teaching experience as full time Teacher at present she is designated as Asst. Head Mistress for Secondary and Higher Secondary section at St.Anthony's Convent Higher secondary School and she has 5 years teaching Experience as a part time Teacher 12 years of teaching experience in Coaching Classes

She has Special achievements which are: -

1.She has been awarded as best National english and psychology teacher award from the hands of esteemed guest Urmila Mathondkar

2.She received Best Teacher awarded from rotary Club of Ulhasnagar in the 2010.

3.She has an Appreciation Award from SACHSS for HOD,

4.Appreciation certificate from rotary club of Badlapur industrial Area for participating in "Capture the Nature",

5.Appreciation Certificate for Guiding the Students Of interact Club,

6.Award of Appreciation for Organizing SPARK event,

7.Appreciation certificate for short film Schizophrenia,

8.Award from ICE English scholarship.

9.She was Nominated for universal festival.

Star India award for educational work.

10.Received women's day award.

11.She was the part of anthology Petals 2020

12.Was also a part of anthology khawabo ka

And also, a part of Ruh-e- Mohabbat.

13.She published a quote book under Your quote 'Mere Sabd Meri Jindagi'

14.She received more than 200 participation and 15. Appreciation certificate.

And many more.

She has successfully made a video for the students for a tough topic like Schizophrenia. As

Schizophrenia is a chronic and severe mental disorder that affects how a person thinks, feels, and behaves. People with schizophrenia may seem like they have lost touch with reality. Although schizophrenia is not as common as other mental disorders, the symptoms can be very disabling.She's loves Anchoring, She reads multiple books, She Writes Poems and Acts, Performs in Drama, Writing shayari Etc

She's fluent in Hindi, English, Marathi Arabic reading. Her Favorite Authors are William Shakespear, Munshi Premchand (Hindi)

Her Favorite poetry: Robert Frost, Harivanshrai bacchan. Her Favorite Books: Tempest and As You like It written by William Shakespeare, Godan written by Munshi Premchand.

Her views of teaching: -

The best education is not given to students; it is drawn out of them. It is the supreme art of the teacher to awaken joy in creative expression and knowledge. Good teaching is more a giving of right questions than a giving of right answers.

Dreams

Dreams are very lovely
As it cares you gently
It is always a fancy
But never a legacy

It cares for you
It spares for you
It makes you hope
It makes you to cope

It's always a fascination
To whom we need destination
It's a care for oneself
By knowing well self

It makes you happy
Without any chubby
It makes you smile
That is always a dreams style

Sandhya A.S.
(Compiler)

Sandhya A.S. was born at Trivandrum in Kerala. She did her schooling from G.M.H.S.S. Venganoor, BA in English Language and Literature from N.S.S. College, Neeramankara and MA in English Language and Literature from Govt. Arts College, Thycaud. After qualifying NET with JRF, she worked as Guest Lecture in English at All Saints' College Trivandrum. She has been a part of many anthologies as co-author. She is now in the process of publishing as a solo writer. Hailing from a rural area, she has always got opportunities to be with the enchantress and the muse of her writing- nature. Chirping birds brought out music in her, Soothing zephyr supplied imagination, mystery prevailed in her writing since she has always been attracted to the mysterious sublime and nocturnal world carved a poetess in her. John Keats is her favorite poet who she thinks is her twin-soul. His words instilled love for death in her and she began to go deep into the world of Literature in search of sweeter unheard melodies.

A Bowl of Dreams and Death

An abyss of perilous waves
Swirling and screaming
In thundersome noise.
There stands she in the midst
Carrying black and red roses.

Silent yet violent in emotions,
With murderous thoughts and camouflaging eyes,
Soul of death, she is, the only answer
To all living and being.

The black rose starts in flame
Engulfs waves as to swallow the dark force.
Amiable yet predatory
Soul of dreams, she is, the only answer
To all living and being.
The red rose shreds its petals,
Squeezes blood as to redden the dark force.

Is she a dream of death?
Or death of dreams?
No answer. But when she wakes up,
Death blossoms with dreams!!!

Anupriya Vijayan

She is Anupriya Vijayan. As a young Photographer, she has got a heap of opportunities to know nature. She used to collect ideas from nature and bundle it into a Photo Poem. She is glad that these elements of nature were able to provide a visual effect in the minds of the readers, thus making her write again. She always wanted every scribbling of hers to be enriched with a tint of nature. This is the first time that she is trying her hand in writing an essay. She sincerely wishes that this book may turn out to be a platform to exhibit her talents.

"Dreams"- From Nature's Perspective

A Dream is a picture about future that have the power to exert force to one's life. They are powerful enough to inspire and motivate human beings towards their goal.

Every living thing develops through dreams. Humans, begin to dream, when he is a toddler. Being a toddler, his biggest dream would be to get out of the bed and crawl. When he begins to crawl, he dreams of standing on his toes. Once, when he is able to stand, he thinks of ways to improve his pace in running. Similarly, when he grows up, he is driven by his dreams.

Dreams aren't restricted only for human beings. Traces of little dreams can be found in the lives of things in nature too. A spider builds up its web with a dream of eating something to its fullest. Upon its completion, the spider waits eagerly for something to fulfill its dream.

A butterfly that gets trapped in the spider's web, will not simply wait for its end. It struggles to come out because of its little dream of enjoying nectar from a variety of flowers.

In the same way, birds too have a dream of a better tomorrow, the reason why they build their nest, lay eggs and nourish the hatchlings. Man's life is centered around dreams. He has the capability to dream big and to achieve it. Sometimes, he may have to sacrifice something precious to achieve something priceless. But not every dream seems to be easy to achieve. Sometimes, situations in life forces man to give up his dreams. But it is a fact that dreams make man equipped and improves his efficiency. So, it's very important to dream big and to work for it until your dreams come true.

Sruthi Suthesan

Sruthi Suthesan is a MPhil graduate from University of Kerala currently working as Assistant Professor at Naipunnya School of Management, Cherthala. She spends her spare time writing poems that are directly based on her experiences in life. She describes her experience writing poem for the first time during her college days as almost stumbling upon it like Neruda- "poetry arrived in search of me". Dreams and psychological experiences of mind are her favorite themes.

I Dreamt

I dreamt last night
Of chandeliers from my room
Hanging above the sea.
I dreamt last night
Of sea poppies
Growing in my garden.
I dreamt last night
Of snow falling on my floors.
I dreamt last night
Of sand dunes
Etching my windows.

I dreamt this morning
Of dying lights,
A Clamoring sky,
A churning sea.
And I, was trapped in a bubble
Hovering.
And plunging, I fell into
A backwater ripples.

I woke up!
And I dreamt more
Of the beauty of innuendos
And finer endings.

Sheeba G.

G.Sheeba, Working as Assistant Professor in Agurchand Manmull Jain College, Meenambakkam, Chennai. Pursuing my Ph.D. in literature, my passion is writing poems, teaching the underprivileged, I love gardening and am interested in Green literature and Postcolonial literature.

Dare to Dream

When Life crumbles
Shatters and falls;
Dreams get tumbled
Imagination soars
To be or not to be

Colorful and magical
Wheel is Life;
Dream a dream
Realize its potential
Seize the magic

Joy and pain
Two sides of life;
Dreams dreamt
To capture the gain
Unleashes the fantasy

Dream big Dream higher
Dare to dream;
Achieve the unfathomable
Pursue the brighter
Dreams are pure bliss.

Dr. Sreeja S. Nayar

Dr. Sreeja S Nayar is a Guest Faculty in English, University Institute of Technology, University of Kerala, Thiruvananthapuram, Kerala. She is a poet, a short story writer and a critic and has published poems, research articles and reviews in leading journals and anthologies. Her latest published book is The Politics of Gender in Contemporary Indian Fiction. Her areas of interest are Feminism and Gender Writings, Cultural studies, and Contemporary Indian Fiction. At present she is residing at Thiruvananthapuram, Kerala.

My Flight

I fixed my wing to fly away
From unknown struggles of my life
Haunted by a weary past
Where none to save my piercing heart
Ferocious dreams marooned me
Where darkness spreads its creepy paws
To devour me with no mercy
And slam me down to dementia
No light of truth reached me
And fed me with its clusters
Deadly demons laughed and laughed
When the soul and form separated
When the wind blows my new feathers
Embarked me from the privileged land of darkness
I flew up to the gazing Sun
Fluttering my wings with joy and pain
I returned to the possessed land
Where burning shackles of love embraces me
Within the old Scrolls of my life
For ever and ever till it ends.

Thoughts

Returning back from the green native path
After a skylarking day
With gratuitous grapple and laudable gray
Found a powerful company of two
Unnatural but asymmetrical beasts
One angelic thought, other a pessimistic view
No curious blinking eye ever saw
A staunch vigilant pal like them
Day and night, they feed on me
Digging my soul and spirit
But now I see the unwanted thoughts
Blocking the vision of truth
Pessimistic thought- the powerful beast
Detained every nerve of my soul
To resurrect the deadly terror in me
And slaughter the purest thought to death
Fighting the deadly thought in me
From conquering my mind and fair thoughts
I jumped into the oblivion
To forget the thoughts from past.

Resmi T.R.

Postgraduate in Literature and a lover of nature and poems.
Doing research in M G University Kottayam Kerala

Evolution of Dreams

When I was a bud, dreams were budding too;
An infant learnt to be dumb;
Learnt one to hide likes and dislikes;
Fear driven childhood days,
Being taught to accept and adjust;
Demand less, voiceless, inable, inactive;
Got in plenty flaws blames and anger,
Inhabited then in inhibition-
Became a kid afraid of dreams.
Later in her teens, suppression crossed its limits,
Forced her to rebel fiercely,
Herself worn a protective gown of anger;
Burst out shouted but not cried openly:
Placed herself as angry teenager-
Against all her dreams.
Responsible youthhood days, blamed her-
For all what she is- of her anger.
She knew well what she wanted to be:
Alas! She was not as she dreamt.
Dreams are now stars to her-
Can watch and admire, but far away-
As appreciation to her.

Vismaya Vijay

Vismaya Vijay, a young aspiring writer born and brought up in Kerala renowned as the God's own country. She's a postgraduate student in EFLU. You can always find her scribbling out short poetries and articles unless she's occupied with her academics. She's inspired by the works of authors Osho, Paulo Coelho, Susanna Clarke etc.

Perform That Little Magic

Living a bold life by exploring every adventure can mould your life dreamlike. Dreams itself can make your life intrepid with infinite love, pleasure and delight. When life is a blank canvas, dreams turn out as a paint brush and paints your life with shades of joy and enthusiasm. When contemplating about dreams, you feel exuberant and incited; every so often it can make you feel overwhelming. Sometimes you feel despondent because of the pressure imposed by the circumstances we live in.

I have seen people feeling down when thinking that their dreams are scary and unrealistic. There are no dreams that are unattainable and believing your dreams are unrealistic is ridiculous. If you want something so desperately, it is certain that you can accomplish it. The only effort you have to put is to dream fearlessly and strive for it. Feeling low and hopeless is normal but letting yourself to live in your dream can turn your life scintillating. It is there you starts to create your own story, living a dreamlike life.

Eagerly waking up to see the alluring sight of sun rising from the horizon while having a cup of tea and leaving your heart and soul to wander down through your dreamscapes can make your day joyous. Never let each moment to pass without experiencing its joviality. Let your skin to feel the warmth of the sun and the blues of sky enlighten you. Make each moment rich with doing something you love. Living a dreamlike life can never make you feel despairing. It enlightens your heart and soul. Furthermore, it captivates you within your dreams and makes you valiant to pursue the dreams that others render as unrealistic. Perform that little magic, paint your life with the magic brush of dreams!

Madhu Sharma

The writer is working as an assistant professor at S.D.(P.G.) Mahila Mahavidyalay, Narwana (Jind). Besides teaching, she has participated in several national and international seminars, conferences, workshops and webinars and presented her research papers and chaired technical sessions too in national seminars. Having a passionate fondness for travelling, watching documentaries, learning and disseminating new things, she indulges herself in reading, writing poetry, novels and short articles. Presently she is working on a novel in English depicting a working woman's predicament in contemporary times.

My Kind of Dream

I have never been a dreamy kind of person, but would love to fall an easy prey to its enchanting grip someday. Dream rings a charming tinkle in one's heart when enwrapped in immense gaiety of a luminous future. Contrarily, it has the potential of shattering one's confidence in one's self too if it turns out to be a sluggish nightmare. Dreams cost nothing but certainly possess the quality of transporting a willing soul to its long-coveted destination. To reach one's desired goal experienced in dreams, one has to sow the right kind of seeds at the right time and water them as and when is required. Dreams could easily be transformed into reality if the person makes persistent efforts in the right direction with judicious amount of keenness and patience. They could lead one to a land of wonders and miracles too as there are no boundations and barriers in their ways. They could be as great as encompassing a whole human world and as short as a tiny moment of one's life. No penny is spent in dreaming but of course, fulfilling them might require huge sum of money which is never an easy task to make. Some jestful people do this job of earning money in their free flowing, easy going dreams. Having no concrete aim in life and strategy to grab the opportunities coming their way, they idle out their invaluable births in just daydreaming. My point of view differs altogether from such day dreamers since I cannot just afford going into a carefree slumber of deep inaction and carelessness forgetting intense pain and agony my birth givers have gone through all their lives just to make me survive and blossom. For me, my dream is not just a dream but a reality to be fulfilled and lived. Only those dreams could succeed in breaking the harsh shell of 'just being dreams' which are run after in full swing splurging the whole wealth of sweat and blood. I wish my dream of such a 'dream' come true some day! Wish you all happy dreaming.

Remya R.G.

I Am Remya R G, M.Sc , B.Ed. Completed Now Doing M.Ed. At Mar Theophilus Training College Nalanchira Thiruvananthapuram highly enthusiastic person & interested in writing . Love the writings of others too

I Have A Dream

I Have A Dream That Not Seeing While Sleeping,
Don't Know Why Still Its A Dream
I Share My Dream with My Heart dweller
Heart dweller Replies " I Am with You to Grab Your Dreams"
I Cherished & Believed My Dream Will Come True Once
Because Now It's Not Only Mine, Two Soul One Dream!
Times Go Around the Clock, Echo from Somewhere
Reached My Ears "I Am with You "
It's Not Towards Me
I Realized the Voice
Oh! Yes, It's My Soulmate, Dream Partner with Someone Else
All Dreams Become Like A Barren Land
My Life Changed to Dreamless World
The Time Teach Me to See A Dream for A Person with Good Character
Avoid the Persons with Fake Faces
Now I Have A Dream
To See an Honest Person Not In Words
But in Character.

Rohini K. Potti

She is currently working as an Assistant Professor in the Department of English at Government College, Kasaragod. Scribbling away irregular verse lines is a compulsion she feels and a habit hard to dispel with. Her poems follow a definite storyline featuring the dramatic monologue or dialogue or narrative mode of expression.

The Painted Lady

"Granny, what is your dream?" asks Samy.
"Don't ask foolish questions, Samy.
At this age, what can she dream of?
She's waiting to meet her maker. That's all", she retorted.

I turn my face towards the wall.
Blotches on the surface yields shapes.

Two tiny feet and two little hands and a loud wail -
"It's a girl", the tedious voice of the mid-wife announced.
It added to the sultriness of the room.
Crawling on all four, baby steps, baby talk;
Dad's Princess, Mom's Cynosure -
"What's your dream?" they cooed.
I dream of becoming a butterfly,
And fly forever,
Amidst these floral hues in this garden of love.

In school, they remarked,
"Such intelligence,
No doubt a prodigy,
Born to rule the world".
"What's your dream?" they chorused.
"Doctor? Engineer? Scientist? Teacher?", their enthusiasm
overflowed.
I dream of becoming a butterfly,
And fly forever,
High, so high as my wings would carry me.

When Prince Charming swept me off my feet,
And rode me on his winged horse,
He whispered in my ears,
"What's your dream?"
I dream of becoming a butterfly,
And fly forever,
And feel the gentle breeze against my wings.

Playing the superwoman,
Rest-less days, Sleepless nights, Empty stomach,
My figure in the mirror asked,
"What's your dream?"
I dream of becoming a butterfly,
And fly forever,
And kiss the sweet honey off the flowers.

Beauty, Health and Time are synonyms,
They travel hand in hand.
Intermittent sights through the window,
Glimpses of the beauteous garden outside.
Rainbow-colored flowers,
Kissed and tossed by the butterflies.
"What's my dream?"
I dream of becoming a butterfly,
And fly forever,
And bask in the warmth of the sunlight.

Turning my head towards the window,
Point my fingers at the butterflies - My dream!
"What is it Granny?", Samy is curious.
"Mama, Granny is pointing outside,
I think she wish to say something."
Irritated look on her face declares,
"Shut the window, maybe it's the cold wind".

I close my eyes, I see,
Butterflies still fluttering in the air,
Among the rainbow-flowers.
The Painted Lady is me, for sure.

Anjana S.

Anjana S is a Post Graduate student of English language and literature at Amrita Vishwa Vidyapeetham, Amritapuri. She has published two papers, "Witness the Night: A Profound Insight into Gender Discrimination" and "Gandhian Trial: The Path of Peace and Glory in Modern Times", in Scopus indexed journals. She is an Artist and runs an instagram page @art_bae_que as a platform to share her works of art. She was the recipient of Kalathilakam award in 2019 from Amrita Vishwa Vidyapeetham, Amritapuri.

A Sojourn to A Reverie

Dream is like a drop of dew
that evanesce to the earthly voids
to become the booze of aery sylphs
at the wakening of morning star

The cold and passive hands of Hypnos
lulled my earthly bosom unto the arms of Morpheus,
the son blessed to bless the thinking beings
to unthink the chaotic melodies of their conscious day

In his golden chariot like that of Helios',
I sped like lightening across the anonymous world
where neither space nor the fleeting time did matter
untangled me from the tangles of Pandora's Box

Raised aloft the celestial spheres,
my heart saw the heavenly flowers and green mysteries;
the fragrance of asphodels, hyacinth, violets and lilies
kissed my veins and healed my hefty senses

Far away he rode
across the glowing world of vibrant breeze
to the glazing fields of blooming peace
and at last, to the zenith of my fired passions

Upon the heath of wild longings
winged up the phoenix of desires
that left my joyful mourning heart
effusive to the bliss of fancy fortune

The shrieking skylark's hovering flight
pierced my ears and nerves;

unseated me from the fleeting chariot
to settle me back under the cloudless sky

For a moment stood I
awed at the bubble-like fancies
and mélange of fired yearnings
that tiered a chamber in my heart so long before

Alas! What does this be?
Reality with the wings of incoherent fantasies
Let this not be a reverie
Or if it be, let me be there only.

Fathima Nazeerudeen

Fathima lives in a dream like town known as the Venice of the East, Alappuzha. Her literary endeavors sprouted from the tales she heard from her mother and grandmother as a young child. She has bagged numerous prizes for English short story, poetry and essay writing at University level in Kerala Youth Festivals, Asia's largest youth art fete. She taught at University Institute of Technology, Alappuzha as Guest lecturer in English for two years. Currently enjoying motherhood as the mother of three-year old, Maryam, managing a YouTube channel titled "The Holy Grail" and pursuing her Mphil from Sree Sankaracharya University of Sanskrit, Kalady.

The Herald of a New Dawn

With your eyes open, dream on
Envision the beauteous scope
Of a bright future, live on
Let not time robe your grace and hope

Let your mind wander
In the wilderness of your soul
Let it pirouette or quietly sit to ponder
To envision your goals and to toil

Have not you heard what they say?
That rolling stones gather no moss
But what a beautiful thing it is to roll
Not to sit idle and to stroll

As Ulysses sing through Tennyson
"How dull it is to pause, to make an end,
To rust unburnished, not to shine in use
As though to breathe were life!"

So, roll on, don't gather moss
How dull it is to sit and gather moss
Arise from that slumber of a dream
And make your dreams work!

A Dream that I have not dreamed
(written from the perspective of a slave)

There is a dream that I have not dreamed,
A dream of desires.
A dream of feeling the rays of the sun on my face.
A dream of feeling the waves on my feet.
A dream of listening to the chirping of the birds.
A dream of watching fishes waddle through the streams.
A dream of walking through the woods.
A dream of being with a loved one.
A dream of being loved and being in love.
A dream of lifting my imaginary children's feet off the
ground.
A dream of spinning them around.
A dream of enjoying their laughs.
A dream of laughing out aloud.
A dream of contemplating the depth of my soul.
All alone in the dark caverns of slavery,
I submit my will, my thought and my dreams.

What Dreams are Made of
(A Poem about Writing A Poem)

When I was a child,
I dreamed of becoming a Queen
From the tales woven by my mother
Struggling to feed me with food.

When I went to school,
I dreamed of becoming a Doctor
From what everyone said,
About having a great ambition

When I was in high school,
I dreamed of becoming a Witch
From all those late night
Harry Potter reads.

When I was in college,
The best of my days,
I dreamed to be like my Teachers
Full of grace and elegance

When I married,
To the one I loved
I dreamed to be a good Companion
To live in love, respect and understanding

When I became a Mom,
I dreamed of becoming the best
And most beautiful three-lettered word,
To give my child the best.

When I started my career
I dreamed of being Kind

Loving and Understanding
To bring out the best in my students

Now when I tried to pen a poem down,
I dreamed of writing about a Dream
Or perhaps something related to a Dream
In a neat, clean sheet of white paper.

Maanoj S.

Many writes for others to read and some write for others to feel, but Manoj doesn't do both. He started scribbling because he got paid. Backed up with six degree on Literature and a FB page with 11 million+ followers, he is now addicted on writing stuffs on relationship for love quotes. tips and few other online portals. He is really sorry if you are here looking for something positive on dreams. The best he can offer is a sad poem.

Night after Night, you Drifted Apart.

Night after night, I lay awake in my bed,
Night after night, I fail to get you out of my head.
Last night, in my dream you were in my arms,
That dream took me so high to the stars.
Night after Night, I brought you close to my heart,
And I hoped that you would never depart.
Night after Night, all the way and all the while,
Those dreams with you brought in me a smile.

Night after Night, I go to sleep with fear,
Only to wake up with a drop of tear.
Cause you are not here.
Now that you are not here,
The dreams are no longer clear.

Missing those nights when my dreams were filled with your face,
Now when I close my eyes all I see is a dark space.
Night after Night, I wanted to be the guy in your dreams,
Like you are the girl in mine,
I wanted to be the one who gave you fairy tale a happy ending.
But, not now!
I realized those dreams were not love.

Kiruba Jacob

Kiruba Jacob is an Editor by profession. And language editing and books are more passion than profession. She is a passionate soul in pursuit of her dreams. She loves books, so no wonder, she happens to be a book junkie hoarding more than 500 e-books. She aspires to become an influential author and public speaker someday, firmly believing that she has worthwhile stories to tell the world.

To get in touch with the author, you can do so with her Insta id kiruba.jacob.

Dream of The Solitary Moon!

On an eerie moonlit sky, flew the raven,
Looking like a witch of the coven;
It flew and flew, all alone,
with no one to call his own;
Seeking everywhere to find a mate,
fighting against the merciless fate;
All his effort ended up in vain,
 adding to his endless source of pain.
Finally, he looked up to see the Moon,
She too was singing the same tune.
The Moon looked at him and smiled,
And then the raven soon became beguiled.

A Valiant Dream!

Lying on his death pyre, he was reminiscing his life,
along the path of valor and strife;
In his warrior life, he didn't have much memories,
Although he had lived some centuries;
The burning fire was rising and rising,
the misery and the agony of pain unsurprising;
Then he looked at the rising sun,
Calling for his transformations to begun;
Soon from the ashes, he began to rise and soar,
like a warlord with a roar;
Everyone saw the Phoenix in his rising glory,
That's all there is to his story.

Anupa C.S.

Anupa C S is a novice writer. Her genre of writing focus mainly on poetry. She had published her contributions in online malayalam magazine. Her major poetry collections include 'maranamenna Satyam' poornathathedumapoornatha' and 'thanal'. She likes to put her emotions and experience sincerely into what she writes. She is writing about what she believes.

Dream my Solace

I like to be in nightfall
Where I could extreme in my nap.
Where I could thrive my dream,
Where I could forget my own miseries
When my favorite nightfall fades,
Where my fancies of dream may evade
But Alas! the chirping of sounds, and the blooming morning
Wiped out my dream for ever.
I could get solace only from dream,
Where I could move like a swan.
No one will come and menace me
In my favorite nightfall I could stroll like a raptor,
There I could get complete solace through my favorite
dream.

Aparna Prasad

Aparna Prasad, a Ph. D Research Scholar, in the Dept. of English & Centre for Research, St. Teresa's College, Ernakulam, Kerala.

Areas of Interest: Digital Narrative, Historical Meta-fiction, Cultural Studies, Mythical Narratives.

Dreams: The World of Subconcious Imagination

As J.R.R. Tolkein mentioned, "A single dream is more powerful than a thousand realities." In simple terms, it's like a storytelling in an imaginative world of subconscious. In that space, one become a character and mostly reveal the repressed wishes in oneself. In fiction, a dream acts as an interlude from the main story. In reality, you may not remember what dream you had in your sleep, but in fiction, a dream sequence is a technique used in storytelling as a pause in the action. There are numerous reasons for an author to choose a dream sequence in a novel. They can tell several things about the character: desires, wishes and fears about their future or past and also it may foreshadow things that might come in the future or to reveal a flashback.

There are certain factors that can help to make a character's dream works. The most important one is the advancement of the plot in a novel and also the growth of the character. Then, how that character reacts to that dream once he/ she wakes up and how it gets interpreted. How the culture within the story views dreams and also about how the character tends to look at the world after having a dream. Often, effective dream sequence in novel helps that character to solve problems, like an interface into his/ her subconscious. The dream sequence in a fiction should be highlighted, so that the reader is clear that a dream is stirring.

Alice in Wonderland by Lewis Carroll, is a perfect example in fiction. In it shows, the limitless possibilities of making connections and observations about real life because the author had used the ability of Alice to get lost in the dream state back and forth like we all do in actual real life. So, about dreams, we can say it is a journey beyond boundaries or a surrealist technique to covey the meaning to the common folks.

Himamol S.

Himamol S is a consultant Psychologist, who did her master's in Applied Psychology, specialized in organization psychology (I/O). She was born on 5th July 1996 at Alleppey district, Kerala. She is now residing in Thiruvananthapuram, Kerala. She is equally interested in people and on words, that makes her to express the untold emotions into write-ups. Her poems are enriched with the essence of life and shades of nature that are embedded with seasons of change. Her hobbies are reading, traveling, learning new things and gardening.

Reach her on himazzangel in instagram and for further contacts in himarose16@gmail.com.

Some Darks

We have some days
Days that we got for.
Yet we let to live
That is with to live.

There are some miles
More than thousands ahead.
Wishing to start though
Let me step my first.

As I let to start off
I see falling pits.
When I stretch my hands
I could see my ways.

Lying in my meadow
Fall in shallow dream
I saw my stars,
Moon and sky in light.

I ran so harder
Grabbed all broken dreams.
I sat to glued it up
Form in big and whole.

I start to travel
Let me reach the sky.
All of my greys
Turn it to be peace.

I Thank my shallow dreams
To find my shatters rest
That my life is not

In just Dawn to Dusk.

Try to relive
In every color and inch.
And break the bonds
To live as own your own.

Dr. Aswathy Rajan

Dr. Aswathy Rajan, M.Ed, M.Phil, Ph.D (Zoology) is a former scientist from University of Madras, Chennai and Former Principal of Higher Secondary CBSE School at Chennai. Have more than 12 research articles in both National and International journals. A passionate teacher currently running a Success E-Learning Centre, providing online coaching and guidance to students. She is also the President of Dynamic Leaders Forum Toastmasters Club (Toastmasters International). An ardent social activist- involved in many social welfare programmers. Social Ambassador of NGO called Indian Development Foundation.

She has received many awards, to mention few the Young Scientist Award by Zoological Society Kolkata, Social Ambassador Award by IDF.

Let's Dream a New Dream

"If you have a heartbeat, there's still time for your dreams"

When was the last time you dreamt a new dream? Are you thinking that it's too weird to set a new aspiration and chase a new goal at this age?

Living in a young nation, we are all conditioned to think of ambition only in the context of youth. The idea that older adults in their 40s, 50s, 60s or even 70s can have a desire to seek new or exciting life experiences rarely occurs to us. The same happened to me. With two kids and career goals ahead, I almost forgot that as a student I aspired to be a motivational speaker. We assume that we had our chance to figure things out, and eventually make peace with life gave us. Then, there's the traditional notion that once you raise children, you live your dreams mainly through them and their achievements.

We often forget that the dreams of any older adult can also be as vivid and bold as those of any youngster. There are many examples who didn't let age get in the way of their hopes and desires. Barbara Hillary was the first African-American to reach the north-pole at the age of 75 and four years later she reached the South-pole. Fauja Singh, at the age of 100, became the first centenarian to complete a marathon and Kimani Maruge, at the age of 84, enrolled in primary school in Kenya after the government announced universal and free education. How can we forget our own Bhageerathi Amma from Kerala, who cleared 4rth standard exams at the age of 105? Aren't these people inspiring? We just need to take that one step which can be the turning point of our life. Whenever you decide, that's the correct time. The only "Yes" you need to follow your dreams is yours. Not following our dreams makes you feel unaccomplished and eventually, this will stop you from dreaming altogether. Let's not regret later.

People who follow their dreams are doers. Doers have more power to create, influence, and change their environment and the world. Being a principal of a higher secondary school, I came across a diverse kind of students and always felt an ardent need to motivate them. That was the time when I decided to follow my dream of becoming an effective communicator and a motivational speaker, to influence young minds. Belief in myself and courage to become a member of Toastmasters International gave wings to my hidden aspiration. I fumbled, goofed up at times and even failed, but did not lose hopes. And today I am a bold and better and an efficacious speaker. Chasing a hidden dream in the second phase of my life, it may be a late start but definitely going to be an ideal one.

Kavitha Kaladharan

Kavitha Kaladharan hails from Kayamkulam, the commercial center of Travancore, and was born in the Panangott family. She had participated in many District Youth Festivals and won prizes in writing competitions. Her focus area of interest in literature lies in Cultural Studies, Nigerian Literature, Diaspora, Postcolonial writings, and Ecocriticism. She had presented papers in National Seminars and attended several workshops on Teaching English Language Skills and published some of her articles in internationally recognized journals.

Poetical Dreams

"Poems, like dreams, have a visible subject and an invisible one".
-Alice Oswald

The ardent appearance of dreams in poetry gives the reader a variant aesthetic experience. Dreams and visions have added beauty and popularity to poetry from the time of the classical period to the present. Most of the dream frame poems reflect the poet's vision about the ideal world. Homer, Virgil, Chaucer, John Donne, Samuel Coleridge, John Keats, Edgar Allan Poe, and Langston Hughes have contributed remarkably to dream poetry. Dreams, the wheels of imagination open immense possibilities of creative expression to the poets. Literary dreams which open their vistas to multiple interpretations of metaphysics and cosmology appear in the literary scenario as a true source of poetic inspiration.

My Dream

Oh, my child,
Here I am dreaming,
Your triumph over the seas,
Over the mind and over the evils of the world.

Nikita John

Nikita John is a soon to be author of the poetry collection titled The Existential Diaries. She is currently working as Assistant Professor in Grace International Academy, Punalur (Affiliated to Kerala University). She was born in Kerala and brought up in Delhi. Mastered in English Literature, she's a proud alumnus of Jesus and Mary College, University of Delhi. She has a blog. Empty_spaces_00 where she pens down her wonderous observation about the World.

When Did You Stop Dreaming?

Dreaming was fun when you're seven or eleven or thirteen or let's say fifteen maximum. Later on, you need to pay a price for every turn you take and every taxi you missed or even the right turns that were wrong or every left turn that left you on the right track. But, growing up, your synonyms change, career becomes the sun and the universe; and even the term 'dream' ceases to exist. The little paintings you drew or the musical notes that took you to another world, or the intoxicating football love that filled you with joy or the fingers that shot the perfect shots and the wandering eyes that was always in awe of the beauty around – all, yes all of them starts fading away. All the dead dreams give off scents of the nostalgic 'you', like all those pressed flowers kept between the pages of your diary. Yeah, sure you visit them, though the visiting is more like going back to a cemetery rather than like a meet-over with your old friend. Sure, you do love digging into the cocaine of the past, but those dreams that you left asunder are the dead ones you buried, dead. Ah! Yes, I can already hear you complaining and bringing up, all the possible excuses that one can get their hands on. Oh wait. You disagree?

Decades later, there'll come a moment when the question – Who am I? – looms over your whole existence. That's when you'll set sail on an inward journey that could be excruciatingly painful on the realization that the 'You' that once existed is dead. It was pure murder, where the victim and the murderer are the same. You know how you killed yourself?

You followed the Pied Piper of Hamelin to win the rat race and competed with the rest of the crowd and became a just one among the many mechanical robots of the modern capitalist world where there's no room for individuality and personal

liberty. You are tied down. You let your dreams die and shattered all the dream-castles you built up as a kid. Dreams died and career/money took its place.

We all are ordinarily extraordinary in our own way. But we conveniently forgot that, and competed to be the best and the first. Instead of chasing our dreams, we started chasing success greedily. And one by one, you let go off happiness, peace, joy, love, friendship, and family. Dreams never abandoned you. It was the other way around.

Instead of walking at your own pace, you started running. Life somehow became a race. And now, you're scared to pause. Afraid that you wouldn't be able to bear the silence and meaninglessness enclosing you. So, you keep running. Directionless. Since you had long bid adieu to your dreams, you start running towards where the crowd is heading. All because you're scared to pause.

Dreams are meant for those who holds single hearted faith in the beauty of their dreams. As the saying goes – Love conquers all. Love is all you need. Love was all you needed dear. When you're doing what you love, you'll start loving your life and love for what you do, will take you to thy dreams.

Dreams are those that you see with your eyes wide open and no matter the age, dreams should be chased around. When in doubt, simply follow the dreams and it'll give all the meaning that you were searching for. Never stop dreaming, for it gives you wings to fly.

Mathew M. George

Mathew M George is a student at Central University of Haryana. He is currently pursuing his Masters in English Literature. He was working as a teacher in a private school and as program coordinator in a corporate company for a span of two years. He holds a Master's degree in Education from Azim Premji University Bangalore and a Bachelor's degree in Science from Mar Ivanios College Trivandrum under University of Kerala. He is also passionate about travelling, reading and writing. Mathew is a well-rounded individual who lives with dedication and grace with a pleasing smile on his face.

Dream A Personal Outlook and Introspection

Life is full of beauty isn't? Aesthetically speaking I think it is. Philosophically thinking I think it may be, theologically speaking yes, it is. Personally, telling I don't think so. Life is not full of beauty. Isn't that an irony? But I do have a solution for this irony. They are dreams. For me at times I hate dreams because the feeling of not getting the same in real life and longing for the same, the nostalgia of those and the desire to get the same will make my mind dissatisfactory. And my mother insists me to draw a cross on forehead and in the four corners of my bed, so that I may get a sound sleep without any bizarre or dark dreams. Because the influence of some people or the companionship of some of my dearest one's made me to realize that those dreams about them for me may not be a cup of tea for me. This is not at all a sudden process but inch by inch I will come to know the certitude of the same. Which will fabricate or mold a completely displeasing, awful footprint on my delightful sweet dreams. Finally, it has always been a good feeling of not being among those dear ones, it's his own small protest in his own small world; and it wasn't indifference, it was rejection, rejection with an element of hate. This can be anything in our life. For me I was mad about certain opportunities and certain belongings certain people which I kept close to my heart. I had great audacity to get hold of all those. May be no matter how much I loved it how much vigilant I were for them; they could just fall over through my fingers like water and nothing you could do. For me waking up from dreams always had given a despondence to life. However, in whatever ways I could try to approach them or embrace them it just repels like a magnets two identical poles kept together; it won't attract at all. They keep moving on away from me. Dreams had just made my heart, body, thoughts and feelings melancholic. It just didn't do anything more to me, but made me disheartened always. At the end the

good bye of beloved ones would be so disappointingly easy and life less; like you leave a room full of merrymaking people, and neither you look back nor they register your absence. So dear friends have your adventures, see end number of dreams, make your mistakes and choose your friends poorly – all these make for great stories.

Rekha Nair K.

Rekha Nair is presently doing PhD in English Literature, in Vimala College, Thrissur, Kerala. She has previously worked as Assistant professor in Universal Engineering College, Thrissur. She has also worked as Guest Faculty in Govt. Engineering College, Thrissur and St. Thomas college, Thrissur.

A Day-Dream

Being a mom is the busiest job
but also, the most rewarding.
Amidst all the duties to be performed,
I get lesser time for my hobby: day-dreaming.

In spite of all the noises made by my darling son and his
sweet cousins,
I lied down on the sofa, closing my eyes and started
dreaming.

If I have one more life,
I want to be beautiful;
not just simply beautiful
but to be very beautiful,
so that every eye that cast upon me
would appreciate me instead of criticizing.
I wish to be so beautiful
So that I wouldn't be a victim of body shaming.

If I have one more life
I want to be rich
so that I can own a room of myself
where I can read and write;
where I can also be myself
without being judged.

If I have one more life
I want to be wise
so that I can recognize
the wolf among the sheep.
Also, I can be a guiding light
to the people trapped in darkness.

If I have one more life
how good it would be, if I were a man!
If I were a man, I will not be judged
for getting educated or for getting a job.
A man is also less judged for his looks.
A man is a free-bird while,
a woman is a caged-bird.

Suddenly I felt a warm kiss on my forehead.
I wished to open my eyes but I didn't.

The warmth of my mother's kiss
Made me realize how lucky I'm.
Maybe this was what I pined for in my previous life.

If I have one more life,
I need to be born in the same loving family
and to be the same darling pet of everyone,
and to be married to the same partner,
and to be amma* of my son;
If I am blessed with all these,
I can let go everything else
no matter how hard my life is,
for I know these are the greatest blessings one should have.
O God! I just need the same family
If I have one more life.

Amma* in Malayalam means mother.

Dr. Anuja Raj

Currently working as an Assistant Professor in English at Naipunnya School of Management, Cherthala. Has a PhD in English from Institute of English, University of Kerala.

Tribute to My Ancestors

Time sets sail in my vast shore less sea,
Deep into the cracked tropes of my mind
It sets sail to and fro on a tumultuous wave of epiphany.
I regret those days I never turned back,
Back to the forbidden woes of my ancestors,
I relished my satiating spirit on the vibrancy of the day,
Quietly time slipped away through my unseen window.
I grew grey, time flew apart and here I get crucified
Waving back to those memories of loss
I feel the pain of a forgotten ancestry
The vortex clicks a humanoid from its cervix,
I always acted like a humanoid, expressionless, unattached
I say to myself,
I was always proud, arrogant, looking forward
But here I am, one who lost the loving ancestry of my blood.
Clinging to my memories I let out a sigh of bad Karma that
follows.

Still Born

She cherished each day her belly lump,
The slightest movement and butterfly movements,
She always dreamt of a fanciful world,
Where her life will swiftly flow with her little one.
Beyond the pleasures of a normal life,
She tried to forget that cruel day.
Her body was violated over and over again
By unnamed men in a brutal riot.
Now from her stillborn life she wishes for a boy,
To teach him to respect women
To tell him babies can be born without a father's name.
That violation over a woman is unjust
That to be stillborn after violation is cruel indeed.

Shelma Jayan

Shelma Jayan (born 23rd May, 1992) is the daughter of Shri. Jayakumar NS and Smt. Anitha James. She was born and raised in Kattakada, a small village in Trivandrum, Kerala. Her elder sister Smt.Reshma Jayan is settled in Australia with her family. Shelma earned Master's Degree in English Literature from Ignou University and has qualified UGC NET in English. She has been working as Postal Assistant in Department of Posts since 2014. She got married to Shri J S Jayasenan, Scientific Assistant, Indian Meteorological Department and is now a happy mother of twin sons Abel and Joel.

Dreams, I Scare

Dare not see me
Rare did they...
Enclosed hands,
All failed to wave...
Miracles alarmed:
Scars still stay...

Deeper, the wounds
Raise from fall...
Enigmatic? No,
Always free I am
Maybe you feel
Sorts that can heal...

Dazzling nights,
Recalling sights...
Ephemeral those
Awesome fights...
Meable minds with
Sparks of lights...

Dragging from them
Restless ways...
Escaping all those
Appalling days...
Meagre dreams start
Steadily raise...

Dr. Annapoorna Iyer

Dr. Annapoorna Iyer is the Assistant Professor and Head of the Dept of English, Sri Vyasa N.S.S. College, Wadakkanchery. She is also a poet, short story writer and philanthropist.

The Prince Of Cumberland

"Man is a rope, tied between beast and overman--a rope over an abyss...
What is great in man is that he is a bridge and not an end: what can be loved in man is that he is an overture and a going under..."
Freidrich Nietzsche

A faint cry for help rendered the air uncertain. It was as if the echoes of the world reverberated into a lonely wistful soliloquy that no one could hear. From the depths of the bottomless well, the cries grew weaker as time lulled the space into a broken heap. He had been a Prince, noble and fair but despair had pushed him to the depths of no return. From the darkness, a single light ray emerged and beckoned to him. "Follow unto me", it seemed to say. With the last resolve of the Ubermensch, he decided to spread his mighty wings and bleed into the night. It was not so simple. The incantations of the light ray managed to goad him to action but his will to return to life had never been there to begin with. Life had managed to play no heed to him despite passing through his body and soul. There were no unctions or magic potions that would do the trick. Laughter rippled through the air and caught the Prince by surprise. Who could it be? His saviour? But he did not wish to be saved. He was not in distress. But the laughter teased him from himself and he suddenly felt a thirst that was quenched before he wet his lips. He knew the answers to questions unasked and felt goaded to know more. He experienced many lifetimes of the untiring circle of love and hatred in a moment of dizziness as he saw the source of his Nirvana. The well no longer had its walls, gripped around his heart. Rain drops spattered and washed him off his impurities. As the ray of light weakened in its glow the Prince had already relinquished his mighty abode and dissolved into the Universe, free from the trappings of the mind.

The Inevitable/ A Sad Tale of Lost Love

A pair of vivid expressive eyes, the color brown, seemed to follow me wherever I went. Even in the chaotic hyper-real world of online cyber space, they would haunt me with a vengeance that could not be satiated. The eyes lacked a body. Did they possess a soul? My ruminations could never solve the mystery but I was never curious to find the answers. I could seem to care less and, in a way, I did bask in the extra attention I received. It made me special, a haloed flower child, who stood apart from the rest of the conformists. Over the years, where I seemed to float from one meaningless chaos to the next, I stopped to stare back at the beautiful brown eyes. I found a perfectly carved nose-- which rivalled that of the ancient queen Cleopatra-- coming to life. A pair of eyes and a nose. How long before I could bring to life the full face? Will all of posterity thank me for having discovered the most beautiful face? Will it be followed by likes and hash tags and sponsor deals? Will the celebrity in me finally manage to put the Diva in place? I concentrated all my energy to conjure up the face. I poured in my desire and focused on the single goal. I meditated, tossed and turned, became a maniac and a fanatic for all the right reasons. I tried magic too. In the end, it was plain old weed that opened the doors of imagination for me. I stumbled and fell and when I looked, I came across my Narcissus. The inevitable happened and I realized I was nothing but a mere Echo, forever churned by the directionless winds of pure desire.

Sandra S.

She is Sandra S, an aspiring Singer who always finds a note of music in every element of this world. She believes that letters have a bunch of melodies to convey. She writes articles, poems, essays, and make them unique in her own way. She had been a part of content writings since her school days. She always promotes life for living with compassion and fulfilness.

Weird Dreams

The picture of a Phoenix bird is difficult to finish. The movement of a microscopic creature is hard to capture. People who see weird dreams, adds up a word difficult to make it happen. It is quite ironic. If we take a look at yesterday's world, people who came up with weird dreams starving themselves to make it happen at the dominance of impossibility turns out to be the history of success. Strangers were the axis of this world who turned every rule of probability. We consider fate as our destiny, but it is not. Our dreams are our destiny. Could you spell the purpose of your life? If so, success is behind you. Weird dreams are those dreams which take birth at the peak point of impossibility. People with different thoughts and emotions were the ones who conquered the world. The source of every success is embedded within their attitude

Dreams alone could not lead to applause. Along with-it hard work, determination, passion, and perseverance lift up you to the hands of this world. When we have a different dream, we might face plenty of challenges. But these challenges draw a positive impact by enabling us to do more. Having a weird dream is not so hard. Thinking differently from your fellow being is not so far. People who had strange dreams were remembered evenly all throughout the world. Still, a question arising is, what is a Weird dream? Your dream becomes versatile when you have a profound fondness for life. When you understand what your heart says to you each time, you will be covered with enthusiasm and happiness to live. Also, the quantity of your approach determines the intensity and compassion of your destiny. Have a unique vision; mark your signature in this world.

Naima Akhter Lina

Naima Akhter Lina has completed double masters in English literature and language. She has an educational degree (Bed) and CIDTT (Cambridge International Diploma for Teachers and Trainers). She is currently working as a senior teacher at South Point School and College. She is pursuing her PhD at BUP (Bangladesh University of Professionals). She has presented her papers in international conferences in Nepal, Kolkata, Chennai, Sri Lanka and Ukraine.

Wings of Dreams

It is said that dream is associated with some forms of psychotherapy but there is no reliable evidence that understanding or interpretating dreams has a positive impact on one's mental health. To me a dream is a goal of one's life. How one wants to see oneself in the coming future. Dream itself is a dreamy word. One should dream big to reach the goal of his/her life. A life without a goal is something like a boat without oars. For if dream dies life is a broken winged bird.
If we have a look at literary works, we can see how the writers chase their dream through their work. In "Sultana's Dream" the Muslim feminist writer wrote about a woman's dream to reform the society. She dreamt about a gender equal utopia. A world without patriarchal oppression and a gender equity which is beyond the violence.

"Pride and Prejudice" is a masterpiece of Jane Austen. In the story the parents of Elizabeth Bennet wanted to marry their daughters to wealthy suitors to make their future secure but Elizabeth dreamt of a life full of love and beyond pride and prejudice. At last, she achieves her dream after lots of ups and downs.
If we take example from reality, Lakshmibai, the Indian queen of Maratha dreamt of a sovereign independent country and rebelled against the British Raj. Though she could not reach her goal but ignited the flame in the mutinies who made her dream came true.
Rima Akter along with her team served around 400 meals a week to sex workers who could not earn due to ongoing pandemic. She dreams to make sure that the women of this community will not be left hungry and their children will not have to do this work.

Rima Sultana Rimu, a teacher and member of the "Young Women Leaders for Peace" in Cox's Bazar responded to the Rohingya refugee crisis in her community by creating access to gender sensitive, age appropriate literary and numeracy classes for Rohingya refugee women and girls in the community who lack access to education. Her dream is to bring gender equity to Bangladesh. She is determined to fulfil her dream. These two ladies achieved the first step of their dreams as they are the two Bangladeshis featured in BBC 100 influential women 2020.

Dream is, D = dedication, R = revolve, E = evolve, A = aspiration, M = make a strong effort. One should be dedicated to the dream, turn around it, undergo the development of it and cherish it. Then only one can achieve the true meaning of life and will get the wings to fly to fulfil the dream.

Arya A.

She is shy to share her feelings and food. Passionate about books and bookmarks. Paper planes and cranes interest her.

Does It Count?

Her world is collapsing
And she is watching.
Watching it crumble
Bit by bit.
"All will be dealt with"
She tells herself.
Tired of her tiring life
She keeps looking.
Looking for excitement.
Even a speck of it.
Oh, how her heart
Leaped at the thought!
Excitement?
In this numb world?
Where emotions have dried up and
Kindness is a spectacle.
Humility, a mere ideal and
Truth, a myth.
Love fades away
Lust, deceit and money
Makes its way.
Only angst and anguish.
Only worries and troubles.
Her head's her happy place.
All things beautiful in it.
No woes and sobs.
Only lies and dreams.
Keeping her sane,
Keeping trepidation at bay.
Tears running into her dimples,
Whimpers blending into her giggles.
Flowers blooming out
Of her head and heart.

Butterflies fluttering around.
A spring she has never seen.
A place she has never been.
Her dreamy eyes blink.
All is yellow and pink.
Glitters and sparkles
Cheers and smiles.
Sweet lies and sweet dreams
Lulls her to sleep.
The world in front of her
Falling into pieces.
The world inside her
Falling into place.
Does it count as happiness?
"Yes, it does", she whispers to the world.

Arsha S. Pillai

Born in 1996 at Sasthamcotta, kollam. Graduated from CMS college Kottayam and completed her Master's in English Language and Literature at University College, Trivandrum. She is currently pursuing her Bachelor's Degree in Education. Arsha is an Aspire awardee of Kerala State Government and she had researched Circus performers, travelling across Kerala. The author is a bilingual poet, Short-story writer and have deep sentiments with the marginalized. Her writings are deeply inclined to ecofeminism.

To an Indian Feminine Dream

At the Beginning of our journey
You showed me abstract visions
About birth.
A women rock melting
And molding another tiny one.
With all the vigor
I kicked a muscle bag.
I don't exactly remember
What all cinematic episodes
You played inside the womb
Revelations about the past
An unknown story
That haunted the whole journey thereafter.

For years you pranked with
My mother's figure.
Haired Red Fox
With long tail moving
Jumping into the bed
Taking her to the forest.

Amma in a wedding Gown
To meet a new hand
I am running behind crying.

Jumping from those dreams
Looking for her
Holding tight with tears
She consoles
'It was just a bad dream
Shashukal!
Never touch my girl tonight....'
The next day

She places a long iron nail
Under the bed.
If the dreams repeat
Red rekshas from
Devi kovils tightened my hands
To drive away the wings of fancy.

Mathematics, Exams and
Fearful punishments
PTA meetings
Face of a cruel teacher
Which repeatedly comes to
Stole my sleeping peace.

Marriage with the very first crush,
Cakes, chocolates and Feludas
Were you, in the growing phase?

Staircases that skip
No matter how careful you climb
 Lord Shiva in terror, running back at you
Holding trishula in warposture.
Faces of unseen people
Known at unknown locations
Brother as husband
And so many shocking dreams
Are still haunting.
Dear dreams
What did you mean by all those distortions??
How do you find my deepest passions?
From the Bermuda triangle of buried thoughts.
Picking up a silly remark of someone
To a grand script that runs
the whole night with
Songs, fights and chase.

Peeing at night in the bed
Howling and felling down from the sofa
In a very wet noon sleep
 was just the beginning
When you grow up
You learn the art of speaking in the dreams.
Beware that is your Achilles knee.

Later you teach a woman
To dream all about her children.
Hot water, a road accident,
Broken tooth
A smile in her child in a favorite dress,
A kissing moment.

She searches for her child in the bed,
As she searched for her mother.
These moments are cherished in a dream box
That reappears how far she go.

Shine J.S.

Shine J S, hailing from Trivandrum, is an aficionado of literature and music. He currently works as an Assistant Professor on contract in Govt Arts and Science College Kulathoor, Neyyattinkara. His interests include western classical music, hymnology, literature and film.

Free Freed Freed

Free Freed Freed, the manacles of pricking reality,
as a dip in Ameles Potamos,
drowned her in vivid oblivion.
Sycorax to the boundaries she owned
fettered herself in rigid caves destined.

Came a many to conquer, to subject, to possess,
in her escaping settlement she sat on "burnished throne."
Never ever renounced the regal robe of purple,
embraced its coarse but silky elegance,
ecstasy overflowed from mind to soul.

Crooning her dream to sleep she woke up from slumber,
still wounded and panged, she surrendered.

Keerthana Rajeev

Keerthana Rajeev was born and brought up in Kerala. She completed her degree in Computer Science Engineering and is currently working as a Systems Engineer Trainee with Infosys. She grew up believing that writing has the power and capability to explore thoughts and opinions that can change the world. Apart from writing, she has an ardent passion for singing.

Unwithered Dreams

A boy of five
Walking down the street
Carried in heart
A million possibilities
Of happiness, of love
Believing in magic and pixie dust
Where sorrows ceased
Treacheries non existent

Time flies like wild wind
Now, a boy of ten
Trying to fit into the world
Confined to the norms
Learning to be independent
Saw everything around wasn't as bright
As he once thought
Through the dark and the bright
He saw the greys too

The boy, now a teenager
Began to see the world in its true colors
The ugly colors it was hiding
The lovey-dovey nest he called home
Turned into a wilted flower
The constant murmurs behind the back
Turned to violent screams
The once calm sky turned into a brutal shade of black
And heavy downpours
A sound sleep became a dream
And dreams started to dry out
Until none was left
And all around him smelled of death

With all hopes dead
He marched towards the turquoise ocean
Filled with people - laughing, enjoying
Emotions that seemed far fetched
Waves were eerily calm that day
Staring into the endless horizon
Reminiscing childhood memories
Lost in the train of thought
When he opened his eyes
Took a deep breath and looked around
A baby turtle hatching out on a beach,
Crawling back into the mighty ocean
A suckling holding on to his mom's fingers
The bioluminescence of a phytoplankton
The fresh air, The glorious skies
The never-ending horizon
The soft sand and cool breeze
The miracle he needed the most
Was right in front of him
When the wind blew on his face
The remorse and regrets faded
The excruciating pain vanished
A warmth filled his body and soul
And reflected back to the dreams
Of a five-year-old boy.

Nayim Nasar P.

Nayim Nasar P is from Thalassery, Kerala. He is an English Graduate currently pursuing Masters in Social Work. He believes poetry is the subtlety that could either break or make the minds of those who seem to embrace it. Surely those who unburden their soul with a pen on a paper will find tranquility.

Dream Space

Mellows of cloud and a moist ray
Awaits to shine up until tomorrow
But for now, this moment counts
Is there a minute or two to borrow?

Boisterous of what has gone
And what came by
I dreamt 'bout living in the moment
Ignorant, the time carries on

The moon doesn't go around
The earth stays the same
Abient to a sleep so profound
Mind arcanely play games

Woke with a shut-eye
Did I saw a world?
Where the thoughts could fly
And the truth can defy

The bright bewitching glories
The dark enigmatic loop
Both at times make a story
Either of falling or savoring a soup

Where is this space
Where does it take
To a glimpse of future
Or to an absurd quagmire?

In the deepest caves
And in the densest woods
In the daze of gaze

And the thickest muds...

Is there a ray of hope to seek?
If not today, maybe in the offing
Gaping down like a creek-
Came the dreams benumbing.

Aravind S.S.

He is Aravind S.S. Presently he is working as a teacher at Sebastian Indian Social Projects, Kovalam. He has big passion in Teaching, Literature, social work and Making Films

Broken Mirrors

Shaded shores to be seen in eternity-
The streetlights were broken; In the soil.
Stars who throw questions,
Like looking for someone?
Where to look for the secrets hidden in the stone pavilions?
There is a black cloud like a naked monster, the sky bursting and hanging;
Thoughts fled in fear and wandered into the darkness.
On the sacred stripped fingers,
You, soul, with the blood-stained cloth!
Seek in the blue curtain of judgment,
Just the seeds and roots of the past.
In the lap of dry soil, decaying emotions.
Life is a journey full of memories, in the bag of thoughts.
Broken mirrors, blood dripping.
You, the scattered seeds of doom
Looking for distance.,
Another war in mind,
Began for the devil.
Another never-ending journey,
For that, let's find a way.
Another birth in hope,
Let the light shine and dawn.

Dreams

What were your dreams?
A house with colors?
A lantern with the moon?
A shower by the hand of the wind?
Why do you look so far away?
The deserted beach that no one has seen,
Have the footprints faded?
Do destiny and laughter go together?
In the eyes, seeking mercy -
The spirits swallowed the seaweed.
Dreams may have meanings.
Secrets you and I do not know.

Sachin Jose Mattam

Sachin Jose Mattam, an young man of 24, completed his post-graduation in MA English from St.Joseph's College Devagiri with interests in books and films and a native of Nilambur, is a passionate upcoming writer. The spontaneous flow of words seems absurd but it reflects strong emotions. With stubborn opinions he is daring enough to prove his points without fail. Being a good orator, he has his own opinion about everything that comes to his mind and is free to express it without fail. Determined to occupy his space as a bilingual writer (in English and Malayalam) he is on his rail, improving himself day by day.

Address: Panthaplackal House
Pookkottumpadam PO
Perinchooril, Nilambur via
Malappuram District, Kerala.
Pin -679332
Mob-8078163310

My Secret Way of Interpretation.

How can someone forget,
The passion and intensity of love making?
The lips that hold love,
The heart pregnant with love,
The pale shadow of care,
The intense hug of dare,
Fallen now to fathoms deep,
Yet to picture the precious time.

Welcome dream my ace trump card,
My teddy of love,
My super canvas.
I dreamt of my dream of love making
Loving the most of the motionless heart
Never else to be preserved in precision,
The guardian angel of my pregnant heart.

Nobody solves my jigsaw lines
Nor no Freud interpret my thoughts on John
Thoughts are buried deep down here,
Preserved for resurrection at the midnight kiss.
Dream, my lord, my master drug,
Take me down to the fathoms low.

Aleena K. Benny

Aleena is currently doing B ed in English from St Joseph's Training College, Pavaratty, Thrissur. She completed her Masters in English language and literature from Sree Sankaracharya University of Sanskrit Main center, Kalady. She did her graduation in English literature from Prajyoti NIketan College, Pudukkad.

Higher Dreams

Gentle breeze tickled me,
The soothing effect covered me.
The swinging of rocking chair,
The lullaby of nature,
Slowly and steadily, I closed my eyes.
I was surrounded by darkness.
Drawn by an unknown force,
I start floating in the air.
Weightless like a feather I am still moving.
I am gifted with two wings.
I am flying much higher.
What happened to me?
Where is the darkness?
With a cracking sound, a door opened.
A new world greeted me.
Thousands of smiling faces,
Everywhere the grace abounds.
No more sorrows and griefs.
No more ailments and illness.
A prosperous fertile land.
A place in full bloom.
Squirrels jumping over the bushes,
Majestic dance of the peacock.
People with peace and smile,
Exchange gifts with others.
The grand table in the middle –
filled with sumptuous delicacies.
No barrier for birds and animals.
All are happily dining in these table.
All are in harmony.
To celebrate, to enjoy, to live.
Suddenly I am tired,
My wings became powerless.

I am falling down.
Bright light forced open my eyes.
Where are the squirrels, birds, table?
Was it a dream?

Sulfath Seenath

Herself completed masters in social work from Kerala university. she has published some of her works in magazines of which 5 poems are in Malayalam language and one poem in English language. she is pursuing PhD in social work, being enthusiastic researcher published many research papers in the field of social work.

Freedom

Dreams seen years ago
By a lawyer without ego
Sacrifices start from Mangal Pandey
Through mutiny of Sepoy
The beautiful Manikarnika
Martyr of kingdom India
Before that queen velu Nachiyar
Become first human bomb for freedom
Pazhassi raja of Kerala
Famed for guerilla warfare

Leader of khalifah movement
Legend Maulana Abdul kalam Asad
Hero of Jungle Alluri Sitarama Raju
led Rampa Rebellion
 Annie British by birth
Devoted soul in Hindustan
Social reformer of gods own country
First Keralite in the Indian currency
Bravery of Binoy Badal Dinesh
Battle of writers building
Valiant life of bagath singh
 The story of true patriot
 Brave Rani Gaidinlu spent
 Her puerile days in oubliette
Poems of Garimella and Amshi Naraana Pillai
Provide strength throughout the nation
Tirupur kumaran and Kanaklata Barua
Martyred holding national flag on hand
Mother Teresa of western Odessa
Pārbati Giri of Matruniketan
Courageous Akkamma cheriyan
The Jhansi Rani of Travencore

Lekshmi from Ammu's hand
The commander of INA'S land
Grand old lady of independence movement
 Active Aruna Asaf Ali
Demise of fearless kasthoorba
During movement of quit India
The leader of the silent people
Multitalented Ramji Ambedkar
Advice for Hindu - Muslim unity
Frontier Gandhi from Punjab

All had one powerful dream
The independent India
Thousands of heroes and heroines
Indian mother land cannot forget …
Hoisted national flag on an August
Happiness of all turns finest
Vandemataram on sujetha's voice
Feeling of freedom on everyone's face
Dreams of Nethaji, Nehru and many more
Loss of life of thousands of patriots….
Salute to audacious freedom fighters
Saving tricolor and being Indian….

Shalu Rahesh

Shalu Rahesh is a student at Indira Gandhi National Open University, currently doing her PG in MSW and Counseling. She has done a Master's Degree in English Language and Literature as well giving her the backup of evolving as a writer. As an aspiring writer, she has published her works in some of the magazine.

A Vision of Life

Let me see what pictures you paint,
A canvas called mind,
 plain and pure.
Thoughts are brushes,
large and small…
Feelings are colors,
Dark and bright ….

First a stroke, just a bit …
Hanging loose the strings of past!
Then more strokes,
 darker and deep…
Connecting the ends.
A mind-game of colors!

First a fantasy,
Then a nightmare,
Ultimately an illusion!

The dream is formed…!

An encounter with that inner demons…
Falling far from the sleep
Catching up to you
A vision of pain,
A vision of life, a vision of death,
A vision that pushes you to put a stop!
Painted vividly on your mind…
Haunting day and night!

Still the strokes continued
Letting the colors loose

Turning the tips so bright
Again,

A dream is formed!

Not so black but brighter…
Splashes of joy, innocent hearts
Without the stain of darkness
Gluing together the black and whites
Stiffly throughout the blunt mistakes
Making it a stronger dream.,

A vision of happiness,
A vision of life,
A vision of an innocent soul
Painted at a corner,
Broken but strong enough to keep you going.

Arsha P.

Arsha.p is a under graduate student of one of the most famous women colleges in the capital city of gods own country All saint's college Trivandrum. She is doing her degree course for BA Communicative English. She has great passion for the language not only to express in paper but also to speak. But randomly pens out her talents, when she gets the time. She has been writing poems and diaries. Recently achieved first prize for poem writing competition as a part of last year's Independence Day celebrations conducted by the college premises.

Dreams

Let's soar above the sky
And dance beneath the stars
Live the life we're made for
Not just hanging out in cars

We are made for greater things
Not all will understand
The chance to touch the future
And to hold her in your hand

Some things are left to dreams
And wishes in your heart
Yet knowing there's something bigger
That we are all apart

So, let the dream continue
And kindle well the fire
To push us on towards greatness
That we all should aspire

Will My Dreams Come True?

I wondered where I can?
because I seen it in my blank space
subtly out of my presently mind.
some may come and some may be fake.
but my dream is splendid, magical.
because it's my dream...
None can ever...
swipe out dreams.
because it's our Dream-
destination, reality, attitude,
magical and splendid.

Neetha Prasad

Neetha Prasad works as Assistant Professor, Department of English, Sanatana Dharma College, Alappuzha, University of Kerala. Her areas of interest are literature, films and travel

Savannah

A pain, shot down my
Spine.

Thereafter, silence...

Another one, a streak of lightning,
Bared me naked

Thereafter, eternity

It was a dream, I walked into.

A rusty land,
The warmth of a red-hot sun
The faint fragrance of burnt grass
Tall trees, broad shades
Mighty lions, meek zebras
Mighty skies, meek waters

"Brown woman?"

I could hear her, welcoming me.

In the embrace of the Black woman,
I too had a dream,

I named my daughters

"Savannah"

Ketan Bandu Jadhav

Ketan bandu jadhav is passionate writer, Rider loves trekking belongs to Murbad Maharashtra. Cares and shares his responsibility and a versatile four-wheeler rider. Loving people and sharing duty is his character.

My Dream

I want to fly high
Without any sly

Dream is to run
Have some fun

Want to be a rare
With love and care

Want to trek
With long break

Want to fly
With a good try

Don't want people of hate
As need to develop fate

I want to live my dream
I want to care for beam.

Hope Of Dream

Life with passion
Full of compassion

Want to be a part
Can't be depart

Fair is all
When I get call

Destiny is hope
Need to widen the scope

Can't make a file of dream
As viruses are in stream...

Dilip Bhise

Dilip M. Bhise is a Mumbai based prolific short story writer. He has shared his writings in multiple anthologies of Writers Villa and Flairs & Glairs Publications. His short story 'Sam's Unspoken World' is already published in writer's villa publications anthology 'Heart Boats.' Presently Junior Lecturer, Department of English, G. D. Goenka International School, Surat, has been teaching (English language and literature) for over a decade. He writes fictional, non-fictional stories, Haikus, and poetry, sensing where you are reading makes perfect sense. He loves to rhyme his mind and bask in the warmth of poetry which seems to be the elixir of life for him.

Contact him on:
dilipbhise76537611@gmail.com
dilipbhise@instagram.com

A lie

How lovable is a lie?
Manipulation is it's a favorable transaction
Trust and truth are the targets at high
Suing and deceiving are the fruits of its action

How lovable is a lie?
it always remains the best companion to a cruel
And worse trajectory to a compassionate under the sky
To keep on yielding, producing and spreading doubts trial

How lovable is a lie?
It keeps track of good and bad
And at right time it cheats by
Confused good has to defend finding proofs on time pad

How lovable is a lie?
Good in confusion gives an opportunity to lie
To get cruelly crushed and die
So beware, keep not only your fist tied for it
but try to remain away and if required flee.

Me-Self

I want to discover myself
from me, apart from being
flesh and blood,
A mere Mortal
Breathing for a while,
In an absurd, hopeless and
absolute unknown Abbeys.

I want to discover myself
From me, besides being a human,
Who is alive on-air,
Mysterious but beautiful,
With brain-controlled
Body, uncontrollable
Imaginations and dreams
Contrasting facts,
And abstract connotations;
Yield sublime Emotions
beautiful but fancied.

Still, I want to discover myself
From me, being known to
Nobody, Except futility of existence
With Innumerable unfulfilled ambitions.

Flairs and Glairs, a platform by a student for the students. We are esteemed youth struggling to carve out our path for our future and we follow a basic mindset Since everyone is not born with all-round skills. Joining hands with people who are born to execute it with perfection is the best way to evolve. Self-Evolution is the need of the hour but, evolving as a community is what we strive for. The initiative as kickstarted by, Founder- Mr. Shubham Shah with the motive to utilize the skillset and talent of writing has now a team of 10+ people who are actively participating into newer forms of learning and discovering talents among youngsters. We Provide platform and services like Publishing opportunities, Open mics, Workshops, Hands-on training. Operating with Brand Name of Flairs and Glairs (Publication House), we offer the chance of elevating a passionate writer to an esteemed author With Brand name Teekhe Zasbaaat. We bring to you an opportunity to get accustomed with the Public Speaking and Presenting of Thoughts along with regular challenges to brush up your inking spirit. The newest initiative to extend our services we introduced in a new writing Platform- The Glittering Fables and Ink Over Tears.

We Choose to Fly Like A Falcon than to be a

Leg Pulling Crab.

To Know More: Infoline – 7781900870
Mail Us At-
flairsandglairs@gmail.com / info@flairsandglairs.in
Or Visit is at
www.flairsandglairs.com / www.flairsandglairs.in
Social Handles- @flairsandglairs @teekhezasbaaat